T0132460

Sixty-six
Positive Ways
of Being

A Lexicon for
The Language of Your Soul

David H. Stegen

iUniverse, Inc.
New York   Bloomington

iUniverse books may be ordered through booksellers or by contacting:

iUniverse
1663 Liberty Drive
Bloomington, IN 47403
www.iuniverse.com
1-800-Authors (1-800-288-4677)

Because of the dynamic nature of the Internet, any Web addresses or
links contained in this book may have changed since publication and may
no longer be valid. The views expressed in this work are solely those of
the author and do not necessarily reflect the views of the publisher, and
the publisher hereby disclaims any responsibility for them.

ISBN: 978-1-4401-4750-0 (sc)
ISBN: 978-1-4401-4751-7 (ebook)

Printed in the United States of America

iUniverse rev. date: 07/16/2009

Acknowledgement

I gratefully acknowledge family, friends and all people who have contributed to my life experiences. I especially thank Morris McColley for setting me squarely upon the spiritual path, Reverend Greg Penn for illustrating the universality of Metaphysical Christianity, Charles Fillmore for revealing the twelve powers of man, Reverend Hypatia Hasbrouck for her rigor as teacher and editor, Denise Bensen for guiding my inward journey, and PJ Stegen for demonstrating our immense capacity to love one another.

David Stegen
Washoe Valley, Nevada 89704
david@stegen.biz

Contents

Preface

You were born to express yourself. You came into this world to work and play, sing and dance, to laugh and cry, to love and be with others. That deepest part of your self, your soul, that part of you that is connected to the source of all that you are rejoices at having a physical vehicle through which it may experience the world. You, just the way you are, were created as the perfect conduit to share your soul's message with others.

Much of our outward expression is an automatic response to our environment based upon the things we learned from the people in our world. External influences have largely conditioned and programmed our behavior; but, when soul breaks through the wall of prejudice, the way is open for our actions to come from the best part of us. This little book is an aid to learning a sixty-six soul-word vocabulary, positive ways of being that radiate health, happiness and good will.

This is a guidebook for your inward journey. You map the course; you choose what to take and what to leave. Learning the language of the soul reveals the divinity radiating from every person you meet. We are blessed by the incredible diversity among us because in unity we experience the total scope of what soul has to offer. The soul word vocabulary representing the entire spectrum of positive human expression is derived from a matrix of twelve powers inherent within the human being. There are a tremendous number of ways to combine the twelve powers and each combination produces a soul word, a positive way of being that emanates from your true self. With so many possibilities, it is no wonder that each of us is unique. Practicing positive ways of being reveals the wonderful you that you are.

Use this book as a guide to personal growth by increasing your frequency of positive acts. I invite you to implement the practices suggested in Appendix C, consider the reflection about each word, strengthen your best behaviors and replace negative traits with positive ones.

No one else exhibits exactly the same characteristics as you. You no doubt recognize from a quick perusal of this book that you exhibit a great deal of soul energy right now and are more expressive of your divine essence than you realized. You are just fine the way you are, but you can choose to bring even more spirit into your life and grow in soul expression by integrating new positive ways of being into your daily activities.

Namaste
David Stegen

Soul Word Lexicon

Acceptance: allowing things and situations to be as they are without feeling aggravated, frustrated or needing to change them.

Loss, injustice and cruelty can be difficult to accept It seems that something should be done to change or prevent these situations, yet they recur in spite of our feelings. We may have lost a loved one or been terribly wronged. Perhaps it is we who have wronged another and continue to chastise ourselves for past behavior.

On the other hand, some of us have trouble accepting good that comes our way. Past wrongs and poor self-esteem can be obstacles to receiving gifts and friendship, but we *can* learn to accept the wonderful abundance offred by friends, family and our divine source.

Understanding the forces behind a situation and seeing it in the larger context guides us toward acceptance. Our *understanding* may include deeper insight about the reasons things happen as they do, or falling short of this, it is enough to see that we are not always able to explain everything.

Be assured, there are no accidents in the universe. All things and situations have their place in the proper *order* of things. Recognizing how the grievous situation fits into our lives enhances acceptance.

Adoration: the act of worship or deep love: consistently expressing love to another.

Whatever we approach with reverence and feel deeply connected to can be an object of our adoration. We can adore a mate, children, special people, God, places of personal significance and even material objects.

Often we hesitate to show adoration because it renders us vulnerable to rejection from the person we adore. Usually we associate the word with deep devotion to God. Though it may apply equally well to a person in our lives, rarely do we place the amount of *faith* in another person that we do in our God. Adoration is only possible with the complete trust which comes from our faculty of *faith*

Trusting someone depends upon their worthiness and the development of our own *faith*. The fact that we usually reserve adoration for the Omnipotent One attests to our need for perfection in another before we can move to the deep level of trust required for adoration. By exercising our power of *faith* we can recognize and embrace the perfection of another's soul even though outwardly they seem flawed.

Love describes our energy connection to the object we adore. There is an element of reciprocity in adoration, and it is the alternating current connected to our faculty of *love*.

Artfulness: doing things in a skillful and creative way.

Works of art communicate divine ideas. Because art is symbolic we do not need words to explain the idea because the art speaks for itself. Artfulness expresses a balance and understanding going beyond skill, dexterity and craft. True artists bring forth ideas from within themselves, see the perfection of creation and through a chosen medium bring it to understandable form.

Any endeavor can be elevated to an art form; it is not an expression reserved for the professional artist. Examples of artfulness can include careful presentation of food, flower arranging, gardening, home decorating, cooking, sewing, wood and other crafts to name a few. You could even elevate business enterprise to an art form through the application of *imagination* and *understanding* to your business plan.

Our *imagination* faculty enables us to visualize the elements of an expression put into balanced arrangements. We see a room, imagine it decorated and with our power of *understanding* the relationships between the parts, know that the results will be artful.

Assertiveness: saying what is on your mind without inhibition.

You don't always get what you want according to the song, but you should know that the chances of getting it are greatly increased when you ask for it. The word no can feel like a personal rejection so some of us don't even venture forth with our requests. As children we are sometimes taught that it is wrong to want things and as a result we avoid being assertive as adults.

Assertiveness may seem like aggression if you are new to it, however it is considerably different. Aggressiveness dominates conversation, while assertiveness encourages communication. In fact, lack of assertiveness may eventually lead to aggressive behavior because our repressed desires can only emerge when the forces behind it become overpowering.

It is not realistic to expect others to know what you want without telling them. It is your right to make requests and express yourself to others by speaking your mind; this utilizes the attribute of *power*.

The most powerful people of all time are the orators and teachers. They use the both spoken and written words to convey their message. The impetus for delivering the word comes from their attribute of *zeal*. Enthusiasm about our thoughts and a strong desire for them to manifest moves us to speak out.

Benevolence: consciously choosing to do good to another.

We are able to select an attitude toward ourselves and others. It is a fundamental step in our spiritual growth to become conscious of this choice.

The Golden Rule is expressed in many cultures. We know that we should treat others as we wish to be treated, and in fact we usually do. If we mistreat others and are harsh with them, it is often because we inwardly feel that this is what we too deserve. The truth of our being is that we are heirs to all that is good; it is our right to receive and to give good. You deserve all that the Divine Source has to give, and so does everyone.

It is through our active faculty of *power* that we are able to direct good to others. When we support them with encouragement and compliments we remind them that they too deserve having wonderful things happen to them, and we acknowledge the good that they are.

By *understanding* our connection to all creation and

the people in it, and that good is the only reality, we are moved to align ourselves with this natural order and powerfully direct this good through us.

Boldness: daring; moving to action with trust in the outcome.

Bold action separates us from the crowd. We express boldness when we step out and demonstrate the strength of our convictions by distancing ourselves from the norm.

An artist exhibits boldness by deviating from the accepted standards of the art community. Whether the art represents the new wave or is merely an aberration does not matter; the artist has done the unusual, the bold, and expressed it without fear of the consequence.

In a social or political context it is quite bold to suggest doing things in other than the standard way. Even though boldness on your part is not always appreciated by others, it shows them new options and encourages them to either validate their current situation or move to improve it.

People who step out front utilize *faith* to blaze new trails for the rest of us. They step away from the crowd into uncharted territory. Their *strength* gives them the ability to surmount great obstacles.

Candor: frank assessment of a thing or situation; honesty.

Without candor, mutually beneficial communication is impossible. Truth is difficult enough to understand without adding the confusion of deception. At best, when we speak the truth, it is a statement of a situation as it appears from our point of view. When we have an honest exchange with another, we are able to share our partial truths and gain greater understanding of one another and the situation.

What is true for us depends upon our ability of *judgment*. Regardless of whether there are absolute truths or not, our human discernment is still evolving and can only produce a truth relative to our personal experience. We refine our *judgment* by sharing and comparing our truth with others.

Sometimes we are motivated to lie because we fear the consequence of telling the truth. In this vain attempt to control the results of our communication with others we destroy any opportunity for valuable exchange. Candor is only possible when we let go of control of the conversation by utilizing our faculty of *renunciation*.

Charisma: the ability to engender devotion and attract followers.

Successful politicians, singers and ministers are able to entice others to follow them. We follow because of their powerful speech and personal magnetism.

There is a tremendous responsibility to use charisma for good. As followers we must be true to our own principles and closely examine the values of our leaders. Whether we are charismatic leaders or one of their followers we should be able to answer yes to the following questions: is this for the good of all, does it sustain life and does it promote growth? This test applies to both leaders and followers.

Good leaders draw from the energy of their followers. It is therefore imperative that we draw our own energy from spirit and be living from our soul before we join a movement while retaining our individuality and protecting the rights of all.

The ability to speak or sing out comes from the faculty of *power*, and all charismatic people have well developed voices. The energy they exude is not only *power*, but *life* itself. Because the *life* faculty is located in the reproductive organs, we often attribute sexual attractiveness to these people. Animal magnetism produces charisma and like any power, once obtained, we must use it wisely.

Charity: giving of ones time, talents or possessions to those in need of them.

There are many reasons people are poor and in need, but none are relevant to your act of charity. Charity comes from a non-judgmental heart. When we criticize and blame the needy as responsible for their predicament, it is often because we fear becoming as they are.

Metaphysical students lack compassion if they conclude people deserve what happens to them because they created it with their error thoughts. Our act of charity should be free of judgment about the recipient of our gifts, including the determination if they need what we have.

It is along the ray of love that the abundance flows from the Source, to us and through us to serve others. The ability to release our gifts and share them with others is a letting go springing from our power of *renunciation*.

Cheerfulness: consistently expressing joy and happiness; having an optimistic attitude.

Cheerful people see the possibilities for good in most things and revel in just being alive. They are enthusiastic in their optimism and can lift the spirits of those around them.

Learning to cheerfully go about our work enables us to do a difficult chore more easily and enjoy our work. Approaching our day with grim resolve shuts down the possibility of joy.

We can choose an attitude of cheerfulness to enrich our days. Our power of *imagination* admits the possibility of good. If we work just for the money, putting on a cheerful attitude will allow us to see the wonderful service we provide, or that our job is a step along a personal path of success. Though the physical reality may not appear changed with a cheerful attitude, the pattern of thought improves and ultimately these good thoughts manifest.

Is anyone more cheerful than a child on Christmas morning? The beautifully wrapped gifts hold their secret joys waiting for discovery. With what incredible *zeal* the child opens the gifts! When we are cheerful, we become as children on Christmas morning expecting to find goodness wherever we look.

Cleverness: mental or physical dexterity to produce unusual or surprising results.

It is clever to create imaginative, yet practical solutions to a problem. This may apply to almost any undertaking, from something as lofty as solving mathematical theorem to the more mundane uses for a bobby pin.

In most circumstances clever people bring a fresh point of view to a situation and being unprejudiced by conventional wisdom are able to generate fresh ideas. It is the element of *imagination* that lets us see non-standard ways of doing things.

Developing creative solutions also relies upon our good *judgment* in order to expect successful results in advance of our actions.

Commitment: being dedicated to an agreement, goal or relationship.

We have difficulty keeping commitments when the nature of our agreement is unclear. Personal relationships can develop slowly without formalizing an agreement and both parties tend to make assumptions about the commitment when no conscious choice has been made by either person. In some cases, one person attempts to commit another to a course of action with little success. For commitment to work we must choose it for ourselves.

It is very hard to keep a commitment which someone else has made for us because the ability to do so only comes from within our own being, and we may not be truly aligned with the agreement. Additionally, someone else's idea for us may be in conflict with our other agreements. We can avoid distress by reconciling our various commitments so that the energy we invest in one does not oppose another.

Our level of commitment develops slowly as our *strength* grows. As we persist, our ability to persist grows. But being strong and persistent is not enough to fulfill our commitments. In addition to *strength* we need a soul-felt connection to our agreements, goals and relationships which springs from our faculty of *love*.

Compassion: having empathy with the pain of others; caring for the suffering of another and loving them.

First, be compassionate toward yourself. No-one else's pain and suffering is greater than our own, but unless we are willing to look at our distress we cannot bear to see it in others. Developing compassion requires recovery from our own wounds by allowing pain to tell us what needs healing. The beneficial aspect of pain is that it pinpoints the issue.

We carry within us the divine imprint of our creator. Our soul nature seeks expression through earthly bodies, but restricting that flow of energy causes pain. Both external and internal forces can disconnect us from our divine source; sometimes we are damaged by abusive people, other times by our own fear.

We begin healing when we utilize our *understanding* about the nature of our pain. Knowing the key to healing, we acquire the ability to understand the pain of others and are filled with a desire to help them.

Regardless of who we are, as individuals we comprise the one body of humanity. Our joy is shared as is our success and pain. We are connected by the universal power of *love*. The love and understanding we each desire flows between us as compassion.

Confidence: self assurance; ability to proceed expecting a successful outcome.

Confident people don't worry about their ability to successfully perform a task. They do not hesitate in what they set out to accomplish.

Lack of confidence arises when we attempt something new, or when we set out to succeed where we have failed before. We either have no previous experience, or that which we have reinforces our belief that we will fail.

Confidence builds with success, and success comes in small steps. If all the textbooks to be read from first grade through college were set before first graders, they would be overwhelmed at the enormity of the task and have no confidence in their ability to do the job. In reality, they master individual subjects at each grade level, succeed, and move on to the next grade. In this way, moving from grade to grade, step by step, they become educated.

Take on large goals by breaking them down into a series of small, attainable, confidence building goals. To lose one hundred pounds, monitor your success in five pound increments. Twenty small, five pound successes total a large hundred pound success.

Consideration: respecting others feelings; caring about the needs and desires of another.

As spiritual beings, we know we are one with creation; we are not separate. In our earthly existence, however, defining who we are is essential for effective expression. Just as steam produces power when confined in a vessel, our soul needs physical and emotional containment in order to operate.

In expressing our individuality we may become self absorbed and violate others' boundaries, or if our boundaries were violate during childhood we may have become adults without learning proper respect for others' personal space. To become considerate we must own our behavior. We need to be self contained and recognize what is our stuff and what belongs to others; we control what we admit and exclude from our realm. Our power of *judgment* enables us to make these distinctions.

Once established as healthy individuals, we are able

to respect other's boundaries. We perceive the inherent *order* of mutually beneficial interaction and act with consideration toward others, respecting their right to be who they are.

Contentment: being satisfied with what we have at the present time.

When we are restlessness, dissatisfied and worried about our current situation, whether it is an apparent lack of material possessions or unsatisfying relationships, we sacrifice peace of mind. Our thoughts remain upon our torment and because of the law of attraction the very things we wish to release come to us. Discontent does not help move us from where we are, rather it immobilizes us.

To move to greater abundance of the things we desire requires first that we *understand* how we created our current situation. This is not an exercise in blaming ourselves, but one of moving from helplessness to self empowerment. We cannot proceed toward a new destination until we clearly understand our starting point.

We struggle, thinking the effort will propel us forward, but like falling into quicksand, efforts to escape pull us under. We must relax to float out of the quicksand and have *faith* in the outcome. The power of *faith* allows us to align with the forces at work and move into a better future.

Conviction: holding strongly to beliefs and fundamental principals.

We adopt definitions of truth based upon personal

experience, intuition and cultural inculcation. Those who are strongly committed remain faithful to their personal convictions by boldly asserting the belief to others regardless of how well their ideas are received.

People with strong convictions may find themselves in conflict with others on controversial issues such as gun control, capital punishment, abortion or gay rights. In a free society, open expression of opposing points of view provides a greater range of ideas for consideration than if only one belief is put forth and is valuable information to those who are still formulating their personal point of view.

Faith always plays a role in our belief system, even if we base our conclusions on scientific methods. Even with science we accept on faith that cause and effect are repeatable. We believe that Newton's apple always falls to earth; do we know this to be true throughout the universe? Fact is not the same as truth. Even rigorous proofs possess an implied element of faith.

Once we discern the truth for ourselves, and integrate it as a belief, we call upon our faculty of *power* to translate our ideas into doctrine. *Faith* in an idea and expressing it in words or actions demonstrates conviction.

Courage: the ability to face apparent danger in spite of fear.

It takes courage to move to action when we are fearful. Doing something for the first time requires courage until experience teaches us that it is safe. Children need courage to attend the first day of kindergarten, but in a few days their fear dissipates.

Soldiers face real danger daily, and continue to

perform their duties because of their *faith* in the value of their service. A strong belief system is essential to the expression of courage. In the case of the new kindergartener, the child trusts the judgment of the parent and takes a risk.

Faith is only expressed as courage when it is delivered with a measure of enthusiasm springing from our faculty of *zeal*. The reluctant child dragged kicking and screaming to his first day of class attends more from coercion than courage, whereas one who goes willingly is courageous.

It is not the magnitude of the deed which is the measure of our courage, but the amount of personal fear we must overcome in moving to action. A simple task for one person may take great courage for another. We should not disregard the warnings of our feelings, but seek to understand the nature of the threat before moving with courage to conquer it.

Creativity: ability to manifest new or unusual forms; transcending the accepted solutions and expressions.

Everything in our built environment testifies to man's creativity. Our buildings, machines, transportation, and social and political organizations spring from our ability to imagine new possibilities and invest the energy to make them real.

Everyone is creative. A soul's first act of creation is to incarnate by building the perfect body and circumstances for it to realize its purpose on this earth. If we are open to it, spirit can work through us to create wonderful things in our worlds.

The power of *life* within each of us gives impetus to our creativity. It is a force, a drive coming from within, causing us to seek new and better ways to express and when coupled with the faculty of *imagination* opens the way to creativity. Whatever we imagine can be given form. This is a key to manifestation: create a formal image in the minds eye of the and activate the life energy to bring it to fruition.

Curiosity: interest in discovery; desire to learn the inner workings of things and their basic principles.

Curiosity compels us to learn all that we can. Witnessing the growth and development of a child, we marvel at its wanting to know more. Growing children explore their environment to discover how things work.

Curiosity is a precursor to creativity. With our power of *imagination* we see the various possibilities connected to the things of our existence. We gather knowledge about cause and effect and recognize the *order* in it.

The scientific method first poses a hypothesis using the faculty of *imagination* to make a guess about how things work. The scientist then tests the hypothesis until the apparent *order* is so well understood that a working theory can be devised. In this way, scientists utilize the inner workings of the soul in exercising curiosity and discovering the laws of the universe.

But is not only scientific discovery, but little things such as creating a new recipe for a chili cook-off that starts with curiosity. The chef imagines the effects of different spices and experiments until the winning recipe (*order*) is established.

Decisiveness: conclusive decision making; the act of making up one's mind and choosing.

So called problems are simply situations that need a decision. The active powers of *strength* and *judgment* needed in decision making illustrate why decisiveness is sometimes very difficult. Indecision is a direct result of either not having enough information to discern the possible outcomes of choices or not being able to sustain enough effort to stick to a decision once it is made.

Do everything within your power to make your decisions the right ones, that is, once you make a decision support it fully by your actions so that it has the greatest possibility of success. For example, if you quit a job to start a new career, dedicate yourself fully to the new work until it succeeds. In this way, you increase the probability that your decisions turn out for the best.

Call upon the power of *strength* to be able to persist in the face of opposition. With proper *judgment* we can see future outcomes for different paths and select the one we wish to travel.

Devotion: strong attachment to a person, organization or idea.

Wherever there is *love*, a spiritual connection exists. Devotion results when the connection is charged with *zeal*. Incredible results manifest when these two divine powers flow through us: people commit themselves to the care and well being of their family, community, nation and the planet.

As we understand our love not for only mankind, but also for the earth itself with its huge diversity of plants and animals, our conscious unity with creation expands. Evolution as a species calls upon us to embrace ever enlarging spheres until we are devoted not only to our earth and the life upon it, but the universe itself. Beyond even the current vision of ecologists who are devoted to protection of the earth as a living system, we shall come to understand that everything in God's creation is quickened with divine spirit. Devoting ourselves to sustaining that divinely created life is communion with God.

Devotion comes from the divine powers of *love* and *zeal* within each of us and shows up as enthusiastic connectedness to that which lies outside of ourselves.

Diligence: extreme care; paying attention to detail and carefully monitoring systems.

Paragons of diligence organize our libraries, manage accounting systems and display merchandise on supermarket shelves. Examples of the work of diligent people abound; traffic signals are synchronized, maps accurately represent the layout of our cities, restaurants consistently prepare healthy food, and manufacturers of consumer goods improve their products through quality control. We can depend upon these things due to the diligence of the people involved.

In our personal lives, we keep appointments, manage our finances, maintain a healthy diet, service the automobile, stock our food shelves, do housecleaning, gardening, and generally take care of the business of living; at least we do these things if we are diligent. We call upon our faculty of *order* to organize the things in our life.

But a sense of order is not enough. Teenagers know full well which clothes hang in the closet, which are folded and put into a dresser, that dirty ones go into a hamper and what a trash basket is for; yet, their rooms may look like a bomb exploded due to their lack of enthusiasm.

Zeal is the other ingredient of diligence. Enthusiasm builds as we recognize the benefits of increased efficiency, time saved, increased sales and greater prosperity. Understanding the rewards for diligence generates the enthusiasm we need to create and maintain order in our lives.

Diplomacy: skill at negotiating agreement with and between people.

A diplomat resolves conflict by utilizing the power of *understanding* to see both points of view and facilitates discussion leading to a mutually acceptable solution. It is easier to be diplomatic when acting as an intermediary between others than when negotiating our own position.

Understanding is insight gleaned from the information presented, and is predicated upon good listening skills. How can we possibly come to acknowledge other points of view unless we carefully listen? An unprejudiced receptivity to all information allows the needs of all participants to be stated and sets the stage for mutual accord.

Clear communication through the faculty of *power* utilizes the spoken word to bring people to a common ground. I say to you what my understanding of your position is, and follow with an assertion of my own point of view. In this way it becomes clear to everyone the areas of agreement and those of contention. From this point all may work together for resolution. This is the way of diplomacy.

Discipline: persistence in maintaining a specific personal regimen to produce a desired result.

Habits are ingrained automatic behavior not requiring active awareness to carry them out. Discipline on the other hand requires intense focus on a new behavior in order to change habits. We train ourselves in new behaviors through discipline.

Quitting smoking or ceasing alcohol and drug abuse starts when, utilizing our faculty of *will*, we decide to make a change. The decision making power of *will* serves us well in anything we set out to accomplish including losing weight, maintaining a healthy diet, undertaking personal studies, obtaining a college degree or succeeding in business. Because it is the power to decide, *will* plays a role in everything we set out to do. Indecision leads nowhere.

Every effect has a cause. Exercise produces increased strength; healthy eating habits result in maintaining ideal weight; regular study increases knowledge; abstinence yields sobriety; and practice increases proficiency. From within ourselves we see the *order* needed so that our regimen produces the desired result.

You are guided by your sense of *order* to the practices of discipline which are ideal for you. Once you choose a plan, stick to your decision until you obtain the desired results.

Duty: carrying out responsibilities of one's position; fulfilling ethical obligations.

We usually associate doing one's duty with soldiers carrying out the requirements of their service. People choose to carry out the dangerous tasks of military life to provide security for their nation or to defend the oppressed.

We are called upon by others to serve them, and when we accept the opportunity, duty follows. We have duties as parents, spouses, employees, employers, citizens, men, women, and members of the human race. We give form to the ideals behind our commitments through the faculty of *power*, that is, we know what needs to be done to answer the call to duty.

Doing one's duty is not always easy. The soldiers who place their life in jeopardy in order to protect buddies call upon inner *strength* to face the danger. The parent who daily treks to an unhappy work situation in order to support the family sustains the effort in spite of difficulty by calling upon the faculty of *strength*.

Duties in one role may conflict with those in another. For example, the demands of employment may interfere with those of marriage and parenting. Prioritize your responsibilities in order to resolve this problem; a suggested order is God, self, spouse, children, family, friends, and the outside world. If you keep in mind the large picture of who you are, you will not accept conflicting duties.

Eloquence: to speak persuasively; to state a case clearly and concisely.

Eloquent speakers express their thoughts clearly and concisely. At Gettysburg, Edward Everett presented a two hour speech followed by Lincoln who spoke only a few words of two minutes duration, producing one of the most memorable speeches of all time. Everett wrote Lincoln the next day saying "I wish that I could flatter myself that I had come as near to the central idea of the occasion in two hours as you did in two minutes." The Gettysburg Address epitomizes eloquence.

When we have difficulty putting our thoughts into words, it is probably because they are not organized. Our faculty of *order* gives us the ability to structure thoughts and ideas in such a way that they can be communicated and understood by others. Clear order within the discourse enables the listener to easily compare the message to his own ideas and quickly endorse the presentation. In this way, eloquence persuades.

Speech brings form to ideas. This is the purpose of our faculty of *power* and it manifests as the spoken or written word. Words have the power to persuade, direct, describe, and define; they are symbols communicating ideas. Speech becomes eloquent when word power is delivered with precise order.

Excellence: performing to the best of one's ability at any particular stage of development.

When we put forth the effort to do our best, we stretch the boundaries of our abilities and grow as a result. Excellence uses an internal measuring stick rather than some external idea of perfection to value the accomplishment achieved in performing a task.

For example, a child's first steps demonstrate excellence because for it, this is growth. We would not think to criticize the toddler for not being a marathon runner, but we frequently inflict this attitude upon ourselves for falling short of perfection. Excellence should have to do with us and no one else.

Growth occurs in small increments. Our faculty of

judgment enables us to discern the level of our ability and whether we can improve upon it. It is important to be accepting of ourselves at all stages of development and get satisfaction during the growth process. When our happiness depends upon a lofty goal far beyond our reach, we guarantee ourselves a life of strife and dissatisfaction.

We get to choose through our power of *zeal* in what areas of our lives we wish to apply the extra effort to grow and demonstrate excellence. It is difficult if not impossible to be excellent at something you don't care about. Do what you love to the best of your ability and rejoice in the miracle of unfolding.

Fairness: unbiased judgment; acting rightly after objective discernment of facts.

The universe is ultimately fair. It may appear that life is not fair to everyone due to our limited awareness of all of the factors influencing a situation. All behaviors between us come into balance according to the laws of karma.

Actively developing our power of *judgment* yields greater discernment of facts leading to wiser decision making. A teenager wails that a curfew set by a parent is unfair because he does not see the larger picture. On the other hand, if the child can provide additional information which the parent has not considered, and the parent listens with good judgment, a time can be established fair to both the parent and the child.

Usually the act of fairness by a person in power to a subordinate such as in parent-child and employer-employee relationships and is given as a spoken directive that utilizes the faculty of *power*.

We should always be fiar to ourselves. It erodes our well being to verbally affirm negative things about ourselves. Whenever we utter the words "I am", they should be followed by one of the sixty-six positive ways of being inherent in our makeup. To speak negatively about ourselves results in us appearing to be less than we are.

Faith: one of the twelve powers of man: it is the faculty that enables us to move into uncharted areas while trusting in the outcome. It is our ability to say "yes" to a situation and move to confident action.

Soul words generated by combining *faith* with other faculties are:

Adoration	Conviction	Humility
Boldness	Courage	Initiative
Confidence	Gracefulness	Loyalty
Hope	Contentment	

Flexibility: ability to respond to change; willingness to reconsider in light of new circumstances.

Change can be frightening because it moves us out of familiar situations. Ironically, change is the only real experience because our senses only detect changes in stimulation.

Riding an airplane, we feel the acceleration of take off and deceleration of landing, but have no awareness of flying at 450 knots through the air. However, it is white knuckle time when we encounter turbulence during the flight. With our power of *imagination* we conjure up visions of a crash landing, when we could just as easily visualize safely arriving and greeting loved ones at the gate.

Lack of imagination causes us to remain where we are and not be willing to change. Sometimes we imagine things could be worse, we don't want to lose what we have, or our energy is so focused upon the current situation that we become stuck. The proper use of *imagination* sets the stage for moving from where we are to something better. In order to get somewhere new we must let go of where we are by utilizing our faculty of *renunciation*. We need to release fear to realize joy; cast off poverty to accept abundance, and let go of war to have peace.

Everything in your life, good and bad, is there because you hold on to it. Flexibility to try new things springs from the ability to imagine something better and the willingness to bless and move away from the status quo.

Geniality: having a friendly and pleasant disposition.

Geniality goes beyond mere politeness and good manners; it is an outgoing, friendly and interested attitude toward others. Sometimes it is difficult to maintain openness in our hectic society because we are bombarded with demands. We find refuge by withdrawing and shutting down.

Genial people, on the other hand, seem to maintain balance in spite of the stimulus around them. They call upon their faculty of *order* to maintain their self assurance and positive attitude. They have a strong sense of their place in the scheme of things and consciously choose to project goodness from within.

Notice how we are nurtured in the presence of

geniality. We like to be around friendly people because it feels good. This healing quality that lifts our spirits radiates from their *life* center. We become charged with *life* energy. We can return the favor and uplift their spirits by returning the friendliness. Remarkably, when people are friendly toward one another they exchange energy and both take away more than they brought.

Group process is most successful in a friendly atmosphere. When we support one another the group produces more than is possible from detached individual effort because of the synergistic nature of *life* energy. The power does not come from us individually, but is channeled from an unlimited source through us. Mutual geniality benefits all participants.

Generosity: liberal giving.

It is no accident that those who are most generous always have plenty to give. They tap into the spiritual source of joy, abundance and happiness and allow it to circulate through them. By establishing the flow of divine substance we benefit ourselves and those around us. When our cup runs over, we create space for more to come to us by pouring our substance into the empty cups of others.

All of the twelve spiritual energies pass through us in this way, and we personally benefit by expressing our divine nature and directing it to help others. Generous people recognize the true source of all good and attract it to themselves, but rather than hording the gifts from spirit, which stops the flow, they call upon their power of *renunciation* to release it, providing a useful outlet for the abundance. The universe does not provide anything unless there is a use for it.

Generous people are enthusiastic in their giving. They do not fear lack because they know there is more where that came from. Fear of lack very powerfully produces lack, whereas faith that all we need is provided to us allows us to be generous. Once we establish the habit of giving and witness that what we give returns to us multiplied, our *zeal* works to increase the flow.

Gracefulness: refined movement; balance and fluidity.

All that moves with a natural rhythm demonstrates gracefulness; trees swaying in the wind, water flowing over rocks, eagles soaring, deer leaping through the wood, dancers, ice skaters, athletes of all kinds, or simply the walk of an elegant person. These images are characterized by oneness with the forces about them: nothing is forced or contrived, but is a harmonious expression.

When athletes speak of being in the zone or playing out of their head, they are describing the state of being called grace. It is a place of letting go and trusting; that is, calling forth your powers of *faith* and *renunciation*.

It is impossible to excel at anything we do when our minds are filled with doubts and self criticism. Letting go of fear and trusting in ourselves allows us to focus in the moment. If we are immediately conscious of outside influences upon us, we are able to respond gracefully, but being caught by surprise often produces the clumsy moments in our lives. This is why being in the here and now is necessary to bring the full force of our spirit into graceful expression.

Gratitude: thankfulness.

Gratitude is showing appreciation for the things and events in our lives. By expressing thankfulness, we show that we value the good in our life, and in doing so, we affirm the positive, focus upon the good, maintain it and bring even more of it into our lives.

When we do something for other people that we feel is extraordinary and they receive it with indifference, we probably do not repeat the gesture. On the other hand, when people show their appreciation for our good deeds it endears them to us. Potential blessings are pushed away with negativity, but attracted by an attitude of gratitude.

Through our faculty of *understanding* we see how gratitude brings us closer to other souls and to our God. We perceive connections to others and accept them as blessings. Everything we have and do is provided by others. For our food we thank farmers, equipment manufacturers, truckers, grocers, stock clerks and cooks. Thousands of people work to fulfill our wishes. We have many people to be grateful for.

It is the power of *life* with its healing quality which flows to another when we say thank you. This is the reason it feels so good to hear those words; they are heard by our soul and produce great inner joy.

Helpfulness: willing assistance given to another.

Through helpfulness we establish our interdependence with relatives, friends and co-workers and others giving outward form to our relationships. By being helpful we make friends, bond with family members and establish our place in the community and economy.

Some professions such as physician, minister and

nurse, specifically focus upon helping others, but all of us carve our place in society by being helpful in some way. The more helpful we are the greater is our expression of the inner resources of *love* and *power*. An attitude of service enhances our effectiveness at anything we do because it comes from our soul.

Love is the inner faculty connecting us to others and is a key ingredient in helpfulness. We cannot withdraw and expect to be loved, but the more we help others the more love we can experience.

We call upon our divine aspect of *power* in order to give form to the feelings of love. Communication of some sort must happen for us to understand the desires of another so that they can request help and let us know whether what we are doing is helpful or not.

Hope: depending upon a desirable future outcome.

Hope is much more than mere wishing; it sustains us in difficult circumstances until they change for the better. Whatever our present hardship, we can imagine better times and keep faith in an inevitably good future; this is hope. Clearly, the divine powers of *faith* and *imagination* work through us in the expression of hope.

Creative visualization enables us to shape our future by picturing in our minds eye what we desire, and acting as though it already exists. In this way we use the same powers of mind active in the expression of hope; *faith* and *imagination*.

Be careful not to misuse hope. If something is really working well in your life, and you hope that it never ends, you have imagined a less good situation and planted the seeds for it to happen. It is fine to be grateful for blessings, but always visualize constant improvement. There is no limit on how good things can get. The abundance of the universe is unlimited until we judge it.

Hope works for our good when charged with divine powers. Through it, we empower ourselves and actively participate in our future. Outer circumstances do not need to control us, because we know that we have within us the power to change them. We have hope.

Humility: meekness; the act of quieting one's ego in order to take direction from the soul.

The human ego works wonders when guided by the soul. It can be a powerful vehicle for expressing our divine nature and infusing the power of spirit into our world, but unbridled, it is like a wild horse with no training and no rider.

To be guided by spirit, we must be quiet and humble. An ego which dominates our being is in no position to learn from spirit. The Nazarene taught "blessed are the meek, for they shall inherit the earth". We understand this teaching by recognizing we are not egos, but divine souls expressing through our earthly vehicles. When the ego is meek and listens to its higher source for guidance, our soul is able to express through it and "inherit the earth".

The voice of spirit not only comes from within, but it speaks through other people, nature, and all of creation. The egocentric fail to see their limitations. They don't know when or how to listen for guidance from the God within or from others. The faculty of *judgment* enables us to see our strengths and weakness and accept help from other sources.

To be humble, we must have *faith* in the existence of something beyond ourselves; we must have faith in God, a higher power, or the god within. Humility enables us to call upon a source of energy beyond our physical world and tap into the true essence of our being.

Humor: joy; amusement; mirth.

Laughter is good for the soul it is said, but not all laughter is an expression of joy or amusement; often laughter is an involuntary fear response such as when a child laughs at being thrown into the air. Embarrassing situations and dirty jokes elicit laughter because of our basic insecurities. This is not true humor.

True humor is a joyous display of the playfulness of our soul. The great comics entertain us with human interest stories containing special insight into our condition. Bill Cosby's exaggerated stories of childhood soap box races, or Lucille Ball's being unable to package chocolates taken from a high speed conveyor belt and eating them instead, are classic examples of humor speaking to the soul.

Essential to true humor is the insight coming from new ways of *understanding*. Learning is joyful, and when we do it in unique ways the resulting glee charges our entire being with spiritual energy. Breaking out of our normal way of understanding provides excitement to our lessons, paving the way for laughter.

Good humor taps into our power of *zeal*. Comics depend upon the fact that amusement builds as an audience warms up. In fact, it is the energy of our *zeal* which when released, rushes to the surface and transforms us. Once activated, this magnificent power can combine with understanding to fill our lives with joy and laughter.

Imagination: one of the twelve powers of man: it is the faculty enabling us to see new possibilities, to construct in the mind's eye things which never before existed. This is our ability to image.

Soul words generated by combining *imagination* with other faculties are:

Artfulness	Curiosity	Optimism
Cheerfulness	Flexibility	Sentiment
Cleverness	Hope	Tact
Creativity	Inventiveness	

Initiative: moving to action on one's own.

We walk upon this globe because of the initiative of our souls that vied for the right to enter human embryos so that they could experience the earth plane. We can reward our soul for incarnating by living life to the fullest; this means thoroughly exploring our world and integrating its lessons.

The power of *life* animates our exploration. Watch little children embark upon the wonderful adventure of discovery. They are full of *life*, have no fear, and therefore encounter no difficulty getting started. Their future is a beautiful unknown awaiting discovery, as can be yours.

Fear of failure thwarts initiative. Our power of *faith* enables us to take action even though the outcome is unknown. Though we are never certain things will turn out as we hope, with *faith* we know however they turn out, we are blessed by the experience. Outcomes vary, sometimes we succeed at what we set out to accomplish and other times we do not. A true student learns from process, not outcome, and is rewarded by having the adventure. There is no failure in life except in missing the experience.

Integrity: holding to one's standards; maintaining wholeness in the face of challenges.

We develop a code of ethics to guide our relationships with others and maintain integrity by not violating our code. A pacifist takes the position that under no circumstances will he kill another human; on the other hand, a gangster has standards which allow him to commit murder under certain circumstances. On the surface, it appears that both people can have integrity in the normal sense of the word as long they do not violate their respective codes of conduct, even though their actions are quite opposite. How can this be?

The paradox is unraveled when we look beyond form and journey to the soul level. Real integrity occurs when our actions are in alignment with our soul urges. Becoming whole is a process of merging our internal divine energies with our physical being, not as a matter of rules or indoctrination, but the action of deciding to express our divine nature.

The ability to decide resides in our power of *will*. "Not mine, but Thy will be done" makes a distinction between our personal will and the soul's will. Our personal will can be a powerful instrument for accomplishing a great deal on the material plane; but to become whole, to be in integrity, we must align our personal will with our divine will.

Our faculty of *power* gives form to the ideas coming from soul. The essential idea behind integrity is that our manifest acts come by way of divine guidance. Who we really are is a soul with a body; we maintain our integrity by listening to our inner feelings and going where spirit guides us.

Inventiveness: skill and persistence to create new devices to fill a need.

The icon of a light bulb shown above a person's head symbolizing the generation of ideas is an appropriate image considering that the creator of the electric lamp, Thomas Edison, was the most prolific inventor of his time.

The idea of creating a lamp by heating materials with electrical current to the point of incandescence came from the faculty of *imagination*. The exhaustive search for the correct material and the proper environment in which to contain it depended upon Edison's strong inner *will*. In his own words he said, "Inspiration is one percent inspiration and ninety-nine percent perspiration".

Many of us have great ideas for inventions which we never develop, but see some time later in the market place. To bring ideas into manifestation we need to decide to apply our power of *will* to develop the actual device. Without the decision to act, ideas remain in the collective consciousness waiting for someone else to discover and act upon them.

While you may not find commercial application for your creations, it is a good exercise of the *will* and *imagination* to become inventive and gives a great deal of personal satisfaction.

Judgment: one of the twelve powers of man: it is the faculty giving us the ability to discern and choose rightly. It lets us see the consequences of various options and make an optimum choice.

Soul words generated by combining *judgment* with other faculties are:

Candor	Excellence	Sincerity
Cleverness	Fairness	Humility
Consideration	Tolerance	Decisiveness
Wisdom	Thoughtfulness	

Kindness: outward friendliness.

Kind people love us just the way we are, openly and without judgment. They see in others the truth of their being and embrace it. We feel kindness when another soul mirrors the goodness within us by acknowledging our divine nature. Namaste is a greeting that acknowledges the divinity within others.

Start by being kind to yourself. Recognize that your soul is divinely created and perfect. You are love incarnate, deserving of acknowledgement and praise. There is no other soul on the face of the earth expressing exactly as you do and the world would be a different place without your unique contribution.

Kind people understand we are connected by *love* to one another as brothers and sisters, children of God. Expressing kindness is one way to "love one another as you love yourselves". Whatever we do to another, we do to ourselves. We are not separate; we are the human family, dependent upon one another for love and nurturing. Everyone deserves kindness.

We apply our power of *will* by choosing to embrace that concept and accept that everyone is better connected to spirit through acts of kindness, To love one another is to follow the greatest commandment of all and fulfill life's purpose.

Life: one of the twelve powers of man: it is the faculty giving us healing and regenerative power. It is the power animating us.

Soul words generated by combining *life* with other faculties are:

Charisma	Initiative	Sincerity
Creativity	Livelihood	Valor
Spontaneity	Geniality	Passion
Gratitude	Reverence	

Livelihood: productive work expressing from the essence of our being.

Do you see work as something you must do to make a living, or are you one of those fortunate few who loves what they do and are amazed to be paid for doing it? Right livelihood as taught by the Buddha views work as an opportunity to love and to serve. We attain our livelihood through the quality of our giving.

If the only reason we work is to make money and

attain wealth, our focus is upon what we do rather than what we are. On the other hand, expressing our inner worth and sharing it with others produces great prosperity. It is ironic that so many so called rich people feel unfulfilled.

Life is about service and when we decide to participate every moment is filled with the ecstasy of being; right here, right now in the present. Don't put off your life by seeing the only good in work as the financial and emotional rewards; work can provide much more than that when we direct our doing from our soul without expectation of reward. The ability to choose giving of ourselves comes from our faculty of *will*.

Love: one of the twelve powers of man: it is the faculty connecting us to all other things in the universe. It is alternating current flowing to and fro between and among all the people of the world, and in fact all that is in creation. *Love* is the unifying principle of the universe.

Soul words generated by combining *love* with other faculties are:

Adoration	Devotion	Sentiment
Charity	Helpfulness	Stewardship
Commitment	Kindness	Tolerance
Compassion	Reverence	

Loyalty: allegiance to a person or organization.

When we are supportive of others without wavering, it is because we have aligned our thinking with theirs. The magnitude of thought power is proportional to the square of the number of minds holding it. Group activity, in which two or more are aligned, produces far greater power than individual efforts. A single person has the power of one; two the power of four; three the power of nine; four the power of sixteen insofar as their thoughts are clearly focused. This explains why compatibility is crucial in couple relationships and group process is so effective.

Loyalty is a choice to be made very carefully to assure that the principles we support emerge from our divine center. Even though we can form associations for destructive goals, power not committed to sustaining and nurturing life for all is short lived. Our choice must take direction from our faculty of *will*.

Tap into your inner resource for guidance to determine whether a person or organization deserves your loyalty. We have an inner knowing beyond explanation emanating from our *faith* center that validates our decision to be loyal. Every thought is a prayer and prayers are answered, so be very careful what you think.

Mercy: kindness toward someone who is subject to your power.

You empower yourself by claiming the right to the resources of your divine nature. This is the path to self-actualization. What you do with the power once you attain it determines whether you will contribute to the evolution of the human race or lose your gifts.

A gladiator holding a sword at the throat of his adversary is in the position to show mercy to his foe. The vanquished warrior can only ask for mercy. Mercy comes from a position of strength but is not a possibility for the powerless.

There are always people in your life over which you hold power, sometimes because they have not yet come into their own, or because your power is greater than theirs. These people are more beneficial to you, themselves and the community when they are allowed to grow and develop their own power. It requires deep *understanding* to realize the benefits of empowering others rather than feeling threatened by it.

With our power of *renunciation* we release the destructive notion that power should be used to control the behavior of others. The best use of power is to join it with others and multiply the spiritual energy demonstrated on the earth plane. This is the way for us to do even greater works.

Moderation: reasonable caution.

Great enthusiasm and lack of experience combine to produce folly. We drive too fast, overextend our credit, gorge ourselves on Thanksgiving dinner, eat junk food and generally overtax our resources. We do these things either from youthful exuberance or lack of consciousness. We sometimes act like the proverbial bull in a china shop.

Lack of moderation is one way of learning how things work, but it is very painful when you crash your car, get sick from overindulgence, go bankrupt or develop heart disease. None of these maladies are necessary if we are willing to let go of destructive behavior by calling upon our power of *renunciation*.

For many of us, personal experience is the only way

we truly integrate lessons, but there is another way. We can learn from the experience of others by inwardly validating the truth of their lesson with our sense of *order*. We do not need to become addicts to understand the destructive effect drugs have upon the quality of lives, but without reflection we may feel immune to destruction and proceed anyway.

Being fearful is not the same as being moderate. Moderation is the exercise of reasonable caution; irrational fear is being cautious beyond reason.

Optimism: holding steadfastly to the belief that good will prevail.

Optimists see the good in everything and know all things ultimately work out for the best. They are undaunted by negative outward appearances and see them as transitional situations in the process of manifesting good.

Our power of *imagination* provides the image of possible outcomes. Whatever image we hold in our mind will manifest. It is not that optimists have no negative thoughts, but they let them pass through their mind without directing their interest toward them; they focus only upon the good possibility which increases the likelihood of bringing it into their world. Thoughts held in mind produce after their own kind, so choose to focus only upon what you desire. Release worry, because concentrating upon a negative future, in the words of Job, "visits them upon you".

Sometimes we come across pessimists who assert that they are just being realistic. They fail to realize that the physical world is a reflection of spirit and in that sense is illusionary. God, and therefore good, is the only reality; an optimist believes this, but to maintain this attitude in the face of criticism, negativity, sensational news coverage and violent television and film requires great *strength*.

There is no point arguing with pessimists or exposing yourself to their negativity. They have the right to choose their thoughts just as you do, but to engage in their drama, or to try to save them from it undermines your own optimism.

Order: one of the twelve powers of man: it is the faculty to know how to do things in their proper sequence. First things come first. We must sow before we can reap, chop wood before we can build a fire.

Soul words generated by combining *order* with other faculties are:

Acceptance	Diligence	Moderation
Confidence	Discipline	Respect
Consideration	Eloquence	Stewardship
Curiosity	Geniality	

Passion: immense enthusiasm for an activity.

We are the most creative species upon the face of the earth, sharing and expressing twelve of the divine aspects of our creator. We, to a greater extent than any other life on the planet, are co-creators with God.

The powers of generation and creation reside at our *life* center. It is understandable why we associate passion with sexual drama, since the energy emanates from our second chakra, the reproductive center. Passion can apply equally well to work, play, avocation and any activity in which we enthusiastically create.

Life energy animates our physical being, but it is our *zeal* which transforms a routine task into a passion. It is possible to live every moment of your life with passion, delighting in your work, family, friends, and surroundings, being joyous just to be alive.

What a miracle are the workings of life, and most of us miss it. We get caught up in the humdrum chores of day to day living, falling into habit and losing consciousness of the wonders around us. We may take for granted even the gift of life, scorning our work and the people around us.

Our attitude is the only thing we can change. Choose to be enthusiastic about the smallest miracles and actively participate in life to be passionate.

Patience: ability to calmly participate in the moment.

Apply your faculty of *understanding* to find the answers to three questions: Who am I? Where am I going? How am I going to get there? Use your power of *strength* to remain with this effort until you discover answers which work for you.

America is a culture of instant gratification. We are so preoccupied with getting and having that we overlook the pleasure of the journey. We drive rather than walk, watch television rather than read, and microwave food rather than bake. Look at all we miss because of impatience: we could exercise our bodies, savor a good book, and enjoy the aroma of soup simmering on the stove.

Patience is being in the present and focusing upon process rather than result. Putting together jigsaw puzzles demonstrates this idea. It is certainly not the completed picture that motivates a person to work a puzzle since it is dismantled soon after completion: it is the process that people enjoy. They utilize their *strength* to see the task to completion. Without patience, we miss experiencing our lives

Perseverance: tenaciously maintaining a course of action.

Winston Churchill once delivered a speech to Parliament the totality of which was, "Never give in! Never, never, never, never, never, never. In nothing great or small, large or petty--never give in except to convictions of honor and good sense." The power with which he delivered the message conveyed his belief in the inevitable success resulting from perseverance.

There is a considerable difference between perseverance and stubbornness. Perseverance never loses sight of the goal. If you determine that you want to fly, no matter how stubbornly you flap arms, you will not get off the ground. Perseverance allows for flexibility to attain the goal. If flapping your arms doesn't work, perhaps getting onto an airplane will.

If what you are doing doesn't work, try another way, but never give up if it is important to you and is an inner drive. If your goal is to complete your education but financial obligations preclude full time enrollment in a traditional institution, rather than drop out and abandon the goal, persevere by taking night courses, correspondence, television or on line classes. Be creative and open to unconventional paths of attainment and never lose sight of the goal. It is one thing to use your *strength* to persist toward a goal; it is quite another to become stuck in a particular way of doing things.

It is through your power of *will* that you decide what it is you want to accomplish. Once you set a course, call upon your inner *strength* to persevere until you succeed.

Power: one of the twelve powers of man: it is the faculty which gives form to an idea. We transform our thoughts into written or spoken words. The "word" is then the power bringing thought into manifestation.

Soul words generated by combining *power* with other faculties are:

Assertiveness	Determination	Fairness
Benevolence	Diplomacy	Helpfulness
Charisma	Duty	Tact
Conviction	Eloquence	

Renunciation: one of the twelve powers of man: it is the faculty giving us the ability to let go, to say no. This faculty stands in contrast with faith which is our ability to say "yes".

Soul words generated by combining *renunciation* with other faculties are:

Candor	Generosity	Restraint
Benevolence	Grace	Sobriety
Charity	Mercy	Spontaneity
Flexibility	Moderation	

Respect: honoring boundaries.

In these times there is a great deal of discussion about being one with creation; paradoxically, our individuality is also of great importance. Our souls wish to create an earthly individuated ego and bring it in tact to higher levels of consciousness. Becoming conscious of our unity with all things is part of process of unfolding.

We impede the progress of other souls and cause them great pain when we violate their boundaries. Honor the presence of yours and other souls by allowing them the freedom to be unique, because it is through diversity that we strengthen the human race and ultimately will attain greater levels of being. Respect for one another, regardless of race, gender, nationality, or any judgment of their worth enables us to cooperate for the good of all. Listen to your sense of *order* to feel this holy relationship with others.

Healthy boundaries are like the walls of a secure room in which the soul resides. It has windows to admit fresh air and light, but also shutters controlled from the inside to block out harsh elements. The soul within regulates the flow of energy into and out of its place. From our inner power of *strength* we maintain our individuality and respect the rights of other souls to maintain theirs.

Be gentle with children; respect their fragile boundaries and encourage them in their uniqueness so that they may develop a healthy interdependence with others.

Restraint: self control.

The power of *renunciation* is one of the least developed in our culture. The key to release is relinquishing control and allowing the objects of our anger and obsessions to be as they are. We lose self control when we are judgmental and seek to control others. Restraint is a matter of staying out of situations in which we have no positive influence in the first place.

Being unable to refrain from gossip, controlling others, being judgmental, telling others what to do, and outbursts of anger, signal our basic insecurity. People project their inner turmoil into their surroundings. It is only by turning inward, and taking care of our own issues that we will ever be able to exhibit restraint and find joy in spite of apparent imperfection in ourselves and others.

The inner journey takes great *strength* because it is there that we confront our deepest fears. Anyone who embarks upon this quest, either through psychological counseling, twelve step groups or personal commitment to knowing oneself realizes the difficulty in staying with the program to completion. Our faculty of *strength* enables us to persist in the face of great opposition from our earthly ego.

Reverence: to hold something in high regard.

We revere the awesome and the precious; God and little babies. Our relationship to the infant is somewhat akin to God's relationship to us. We are connected through *love* and animated by *life*. We sustain and nurture the baby just as our Father/Mother God sustains and nurtures us.

We can learn much about our relationship to God from our interactions with children, but we are not limited to that. We can esteem all creation with reverence for life. Adults young and old, people of any color, men and women, Christians, Buddhists, Moslems and atheists are God's precious children deserving our reverence.

You are God's perfect child worthy of self respect and reverence. Your being here and now is an awesome and precious gift of *life* possible from God's example of *love*. You perpetuate this wonderful gift extending it to every living thing on the face of the earth by calling upon your own powers of *love* and *life*.

Sentiment: affection for another; shared joy.

We feel sentimental toward those people and places to which we are attached not only through a heart connection, but also the symbolism they represent. Perhaps we see a film or experience a place or recognize a person whose image touches us deeply, but because it is for no apparent reason we explain it as sentiment.

Our soul carries within it knowledge of past, present and future lives. We feel sentimental when people, places and events trigger soul memory that strikes a chord within us releasing energy expressed as tender feelings. The connection is made through symbolic imagery perceived by our power of *imagination*.

Evolution of consciousness comes about by discovery of our connections. We become aware in this instance of our connection to our past and future and discover the continuity of our own existence. We have neither beginning nor ending, exist in all time and space, and are one with the all; but, we only discover this in small glimpses we know as sentiment. Ultimately we shall become totally aware of the continuity of all existence and sentiment will blend into the ecstasy of being.

Love is the inner faculty connecting us to all other

creation and it is through this divine power that we enter the heavenly mansion.

Sincerity: honesty in the expression of our feelings.

All people have a right to express their feelings, but unfortunately we are taught at a very early age to repress many of them. Less than a generation ago, children were "to be seen and not heard". What a tragic loss to the adult world when we suppress the enthusiasm and wisdom of our young ones. The child's huge loss is its natural connection to its soul. Some of us spend an entire lifetime trying to re-establish contact with that divine part of ourselves which was severed within our seventh year of life.

Indeed, feelings are messages sent from our higher self as guidance to our mortal self. When sincere, we allow true feelings to guide our actions; it is done openly and honestly.

There may be dangerous people in your world who would strike out against you if you were to express openly and honestly. Never remain in a situation where you are subject to abuse from another. It may have been necessary in your childhood to cover up who you are and repress your desires in order to survive, but as an adult you can release hurtful people to their higher good and get them out of your life. Your feelings are your own, and you have the right to sincerely express them.

Use your inner faculty of *judgment* to know what is right for you. Allow the *life* principle to animate your expression as you are sincere.

Sobriety: austerity; choosing to forgo a thing or action for a predetermined purpose.

Sobriety is characterized by clarity of choices in our conduct. We are out of control when we are unable to satisfy our quest for more food, alcohol, drugs, sex, or work. None of these things in moderation are unhealthy, but in excess are destructive forces.

Addiction presents an opportunity to bring forth the energy of our soul and express it as sobriety. The first step of Twelve Step Programs is to admit that we are powerless over our addictions. We are only powerless because we have not contacted our higher self and brought forth its power. The ability to control our behavior comes from our divine nature, specifically the faculties of *will* and *renunciation*.

When we decide to change a destructive habit, the faculty of *will* is expressed. We usually understand that we need will power to curb our appetite for harmful substances and often chastise ourselves for not having enough. Actually though, westerners are generally quite strong willed, but *will* alone cannot change a habit.

The ability to release and let go, the ability to say no comes from our power of *renunciation*. It is through the combination of the power to decide, and the power to say no that we initiate release from addictive behavior and truly become sober.

Spontaneity: a self directed but non-reasoned behavior.

We are steeped in the power of logic and the scientific method to such a great extent that many of us are unable to set aside our critical faculty and go with the flow. We come to believe that we must visualize, plan and control every aspect of our lives. In our zeal to take charge of our lives, we forget to allow soul participation; we act from intellect and limit our encounters by the scope of our personal abilities.

The metaphysical teaching that thoughts manifest is solace to us who wish to be in control. It seems that if we can monitor our thoughts and flood our minds with positive affirmations, then our lives will straighten out. That will not work if our need to be in control comes from fear and lack of trust. When fear motivates us, we remain strongly connected to what we fear and thus keep it in our lives.

Only by letting go of judgment of good and bad through our power of *renunciation* are we able to release control and allow *life* to happen through us. That wonderful energy animating us, radiating from our *life* center is clearly demonstrated when we are spontaneous. Spontaneity only occurs when we set our analysis aside, release control and live life naturally. Take the advice of Bobby McFarren's song to become more spontaneous; "Don't worry, be happy!"

Stewardship: caretaking; maintaining and nurturing that which we wish to utilize.

It is a natural phenomenon that everything breaks down and returns to the elements from which it was created unless there is an ongoing stream of energy to support its existence. Our attention sustains form; whatever we ignore disintegrates. Stewardship is the act of taking care of and maintaining the things in our world.

What in your life is falling apart; your property,

finances, career, relationships or health? Without your continued input of *love* energy, you cannot remain connected to these things, for love is what connects all things. Look around and see what in your world is in the best condition; that symbolizes what you most love.

Stewardship is putting your *love* into your property, relationships, body, mind and world; it is being in right relationship with all things.

Everything we have in our lives comes from God whether we know it or not. Taking care of God's creations is Holy Communion and there is no thing which is not worthy of our care. It is our inner faculty of *order* showing us the relationship among all things in the manifest universe and guiding us as co-creators with God in sustaining it.

Strength: one of the twelve powers of man: it is the faculty enabling us to persist and to do. It is our ability to sustain effort in the face of apparent opposition.

Soul words generated by combining *strength* with other faculties are:

Boldness	Optimism	Restraint
Commitment	Patience	Valor
Decisiveness	Perseverance	Vigor
Duty	Respect	

Tact: taking into account audience sensitivity before speaking.

To effectively communicate requires an understanding of your audience. It is through our faculty of *imagination* that we are able to hear our delivery from the listener's point of view.

It is a rare person who has reached adulthood without developing emotional buttons along the way. Our buttons cause us to dig in and defend ourselves and even those who acknowledge their buttons do not know how to diffuse their effect. This is also true for our audience; tactful people sense how their audience will respond and avoid these triggers. Their speech is effective because the power of their words is not wasted overcoming the ingrained resistance of their audience.

By empathizing with others through the use of *imagination*, the tactful person respects their right to make their own decisions. Their communication is non-threatening and the audience is more likely to be receptive to their words.

The energy of our voice comes from our *power* center. By combining *power* with *imagination* we become tactful communicators.

Thoughtfulness: well considered action or position.

Have you ever noticed how some people are able to see the larger picture and transcend common knowledge? This is not necessarily a matter of intellect, because some of our most brilliant people become mesmerized by minutia. As long as we only function in the world of form we are limited to the reality as perceived by our five senses.

By tapping into our divine powers we enlarge our understanding of what is. Our power of *judgment* surveys the situation showing us the possibilities and our *will* helps us choose what we desire. If we leave discrimination and choosing only to our ego, our actions can be thoughtless because ego is driven by programming; we project our anger, envy and low esteem into the outer world and it is mirrored back to us. We do better if we train our egos to respond to our soul.

Mirrors are the tools of an illusionist; they do not reflect reality. Spirit is the only reality and manifestations are symbolic reflections of spirit. To become thoughtful is to connect with your divine nature and project its truth into the world. When we do this, illusion giving rise to anger and hatred dissipates and love prevails.

Tolerance: respecting the beliefs and behavior of others.

Bigotry and intolerance are the misuse of the power of *judgment*. The Nazarene taught "Judge not, lest thou be judged," meaning that when we label something as good or bad, we place limits upon it and therefore limit ourselves. By remaining open and receptive to all of God's gifts, to all that is, we are able to expand our consciousness and transcend apparent duality. God is all that is, and God is good.

The only sin is restriction. When we reject other people because of their race, gender, nationality and even for abhorrent behavior, we reject the part of ourselves that is reflected in them. This type of judgment separates us from our creator and Its universe. We must become tolerant of what is and rejoice in the miracle of it if we are to go beyond earthbound consciousness. We are connected to one another through the power of *love*.

The right use of the power of *judgment* functions in an atmosphere of unprejudiced receptivity. It enables us to see things as they are without personalized coloration.

When our thinking is clear, unclouded by ego's fear and judgment, we may embrace all people as brothers and sisters, loving them as our selves.

Understanding: one of the twelve powers of man: it is the faculty giving us the ability to discern the fundamental truth of cause and effect. When we see the things and events in our world as symbolic of deeper meaning, understanding is our ability to get to that meaning.

Soul words generated by combining *understanding* with other faculties are:

Acceptance	Diplomacy	Patience
Artfulness	Gratitude	Willingness
Compassion	Humor	Wisdom
Contentment	Mercy	

Valor: courage with dignity; poise in the face of opposition.

The archetypical warrior symbolizes strength in the face of adversity. He pits his very life energy against the enemy in mortal combat, risking all for victory. We see valor not only in soldiers, but in all who face their own demons with dignity.

The act of Rosa Parks, holding her position to sit up front on a bus in the face of Jim Crow showed great valor, as did the civil rights marchers in the sixties. What courage and poise so many of the elderly exhibit as they face old age and debility. Our greatest fears are the ones we carry within and the decision to meet them face on through professional counseling is also a tremendous act of valor.

It is the *life* energy itself that we struggle to express, that divine aspect of ourselves urging our animation. The ill who will not give up, the persecuted who fight for freedom and the repressed, moving to speak out, seek to openly express *life*.

When the flame of life is most dim, it is through our faculty of *strength* that we persist. Combining the two energies of life and strength produces valorous deeds and acts of heroism.

Vigor: strong physical or mental activity.

Vigorous people are persistent and enthusiastic. Well conditioned athletes, people fighting the elements, and mountain climbers exhibit physical vigor while negotiators, business people and scientific researchers display mental vigor.

We sometimes feel that we just do not have the strength to continue on a chosen path, but it is more likely a lack of enthusiasm. If you literally light a fire under someone, regardless of how tired they feel, they find the strength to run. The key is finding the right motivation.

To embark upon a task tap into your power of zeal and find reasons to be enthusiastic about getting started. After getting started our ability to persist, our endurance, comes from our faculty of *strength*. The two powers working in concert overcome inertia and sustain momentum to accomplish a given task with vigor.

Volition: the act of free choice.

Volition is about self empowerment. We are endowed by our creator with the right of free choice, but if we abdicate, someone will choose for us. If we feel powerless and victimized when others tell us what to do it is because we have given up or been stripped of our rights.

That we must make choices is a basic rule in the game of life. Choices cannot be avoided, so why not choose what you desire? If you are in an abusive situation either at home or at work, or you feel powerless or victimized in any way, ask what decisions you made that resulted in the situation, and what you can do about it.

The greatest tool for taking charge of your life is to say "I have something to say about that," and then act upon it. While our ability to decide comes from our power of *will*, it is difficult to exercise without a modicum of *zeal*. It is extremely difficult to be enthusiastic about choices other people have made for you, so get behind your desires and start making your own choices. Charge your decisions with *zeal* and anything is possible.

Will: one of the twelve powers of man: it is the faculty giving us the ability to decide. It is through the use of will that we choose what it is we want.

Soul words generated by combining *will* with other faculties are:

Determination	Livelihood	Sobriety
Thoughtfulness	Discipline	Loyalty
Willingness	Inventiveness	Perseverance
Volition	Kindness	

Willingness: gladly accepting.

Opportunity abounds for those who greet it with open arms. Why is it that so many of us are reluctant to participate in life? Has it caused us that much pain? We develop coping mechanisms during childhood that hinder our growth when carried into adulthood. We know that when we are receptive, we become vulnerable to hurt, but guarding against hurt cuts us off from pleasure.

One escape from this dilemma is to go inward and tap our power of *understanding*. This inner knowing casts light upon our painful memories, allowing us to release them and see the lack of relevance to our current situation. Through understanding we come to know the truth of our being as children of God, precious and deserving in every way. We relinquish our judgment of the past as bad and understand the good which has come from it. After all, who you are today is partly a result of those experiences.

Stepping into willingness, that place of joyous participation and acceptance of what is offered sets us free to enjoy all that God and man have to offer. This is a place where we have options; we can utilize our power of *will* and decide to receive or not. What more can we ask of life than the opportunity to fully participate? What a gift we give ourselves when we accept the challenge? It is God's province to offer life; it is ours to accept.

Wisdom: good judgment; profound understanding.

Wisdom is mature and calm, drawing its energy from our divine faculties of *judgment* and *understanding*. It is born not of emotion, but of deep feeling. Emotion is of the ego, feeling comes from the soul. The shaman, priest, priestess and teacher know the wisdom of their own souls and use the spiritual knowledge emitted from their divinity to guide their affairs.

Our great capacity for wisdom comes from an inner knowing. Prayer and meditation are useful techniques to accomplish this for they quiet the mind and prepare us to listen. We should listen for that still small voice speaking to us in prayer, for it is the guidance we seek. In time, we learn to listen to this intuition and follow its guidance in all that we do, knowing it directs us perfectly along our way. Our soul guides us to make wise decisions.

Zeal: one of the twelve powers of man: it is the faculty of motivation. It is the spark of enthusiasm that inspires us to action. It plays a role in most outer expression, for without interest in expressing ourselves we would become only observers of life.

Soul words generated by combining *zeal* with other faculties are:

Assertiveness	Diligence	Passion
Cheerfulness	Excellence	Vigor
Courage	Generosity	Volition
Devotion	Humor	

Appendix A
Soul Word Synonyms

While the words in the Soul Word Dictionary cover the entire range of expression resulting from various combinations of twelve powers, there are many positive traits which are not specifically discussed. The following positive behaviors are also soul directed and are synonymous with soul words or are combinations of two or more soul words. Synonyms and related words are listed for your reference.

Amiability: cheerfulness, geniality, benevolence, thoughtfulness

Appreciation: gratitude

Bravery: boldness, courage

Calmness: acceptance, contentment

Charm: gracefulness, geniality

Cooperation: benevolence, flexibility, respect, tact

Concern: prudence, stewardship

Conscientiousness: diligence, duty, thoughtfulness, wisdom

Craftiness: cleverness, creativity

Daring: boldness

Discretion: moderation

Earnestness: conviction, sincerity

Enterprise: initiative, volition

Enthusiasm: zeal

Friendliness: geniality, helpfulness

Forgiveness: acceptance, compassion, kindness, tolerance, mercy

Gaiety: cheerfulness, humor, optimism, passion

Gallantry: consideration, gracefulness, respect, sentiment

Grief: passion, respect, sentiment, sincerity

Honesty: candor, fairness, integrity

Hospitality: gracefulness, kindness, stewardship

Imperturbability: acceptance, confidence, restraint, tolerance

Industriousness: commitment, duty, passion

Inquisitiveness: curiosity

Judiciousness: moderation

Modesty: humility, respect

Obedience: devotion, loyalty, reverence

Openness: flexibility, willingness

Philanthropy: charity, generosity

Playfulness: cheerfulness, geniality, humor, inventiveness, spontaneity, vigor

Pride: excellence, stewardship

Propriety: moderation, sobriety

Receptiveness: flexibility, willingness

Reliability: commitment, diligence, helpfulness

Resoluteness: conviction, decisiveness, volition

Remorse: candor, fairness, humility

Shyness: humility, respect, tact

Spunk: boldness, initiative, optimism, vigor

Tenacity: conviction, perseverance

Toughness: courage, diligence, vigor

Trust: faith

Vivaciousness: charisma, passion

Warmhearted: benevolence, compassion, kindness

Wit: humor

Appendix B

Antonyms to Negative Behaviour

The only value in looking at negative behavior is to develop an awareness of its presence in your life. You cannot transform yourself to full soul expression by denying that you have destructive traits, but neither can you overcome them by directly working on them because whatever you focus upon grows; therefore, when you become aware of an unhealthy trait remind yourself that you have the power to choose differently: you can replace a negative trait only by focusing upon its antithesis.

If you possess any of the following traits, look at it as an opportunity to bring forth the language of your soul by studying the suggested ways of being following it.

Aggressiveness: assertiveness, contentment, geniality, humility, respect

Ambivalence: commitment, decisiveness

Anger: acceptance, contentment, patience, tolerance

Antagonism: benevolence, cheerfulness, flexibility

Arrogance: consideration, eloquence, geniality, humility, thoughtfulness

Bigotry: acceptance, charity, kindness, respect, tolerance

Boredom: contentment, curiosity, initiative, willingness

Bossiness: assertiveness, charisma, diplomacy, gracefulness, tact

Bitterness: acceptance, benevolence, gracefulness, hope, tolerance

Cheating: excellence, conviction, integrity, respect, fairness

Compulsiveness: decisiveness, diligence, discipline, restraint, sobriety

Cowardice: boldness, confidence, courage, gracefulness, valor

Criticism: acceptance, compassion, generosity, helpfulness, kindness, stewardship

Cruelty: compassion, kindness, respect, thoughtfulness, mercy

Denial: acceptance, courage, hope, willingness

Destructiveness: gratitude, respect, stewardship, thoughtfulness

Despair: acceptance, cheerfulness, gracefulness, gratitude, humility, hope, optimism, perseverance, willingness

Disrespect: consideration, devotion, gratitude, helpfulness, stewardship, kindness, respect, reverence

Distrust: boldness, confidence, gracefulness, tolerance, willingness, loyalty

Drollness: artfulness, creativity, humor, inventiveness, passion, spontaneity

Egotism: contentment, devotion, gracefulness, humility, reverence, wisdom

Fanaticism: charisma, contentment, conviction, gracefulness, humility, moderation, wisdom

Fear: boldness, confidence, courage, eloquence, valor, willingness

Foolishness: cleverness, excellence, diligence, moderation, wisdom

Greed: charity, fairness, restraint, sobriety

Guilt: acceptance, charity, compassion, humility, mercy, stewardship

Hatred: acceptance, benevolence, compassion, fairness, mercy, tolerance

Hopelessness: gracefulness, hope, patience, perseverance

Hostility: benevolence, cheerfulness, eloquence, geniality, tolerance

Hypochondria: gracefulness, hope, humility, optimism, sobriety

Impatience: contentment, discipline, gracefulness, patience, perseverance, restraint, tolerance

Indecision: commitment, conviction, decisiveness, duty, initiative, volition

Indifference: artfulness, curiosity, gratitude, inventiveness, passion, vigor, willingness

Insecurity: boldness, confidence, courage, gracefulness, hope, optimism, spontaneity, willingness

Intolerance: acceptance, benevolence, diplomacy, compassion, geniality, respect, tact

Irresponsibility: excellence, diligence, helpfulness, integrity, respect, stewardship

Jealousy: adoration, confidence, devotion, generosity, gracefulness, kindness, moderation

Loathing: adoration, charity, contentment, flexibility, mercy, restraint

Laziness: cleverness, discipline, excellence, initiative, livelihood, spontaneity, vigor

Lying: assertiveness, candor, consideration, conviction, integrity, sincerity

Lust: contentment, discipline, integrity, moderation, restraint, sobriety

Meanness: benevolence, compassion, fairness, kindness, mercy

Melancholy: boldness, cheerfulness, commitment, gratitude, optimism, volition

Perfectionism: excellence, gracefulness, flexibility, sobriety

Pessimism: contentment, hope, humor, initiative, optimism

Possessiveness: contentment, generosity, gracefulness, restraint,

Pride: humility, restraint, wisdom

Prejudice: acceptance, charity, kindness, respect, tolerance

Procrastination: assertiveness, commitment, confidence, courage, creativity, initiative, perseverance, stewardship

Resentment: acceptance, contentment, gracefulness, willingness

Rudeness: consideration, diplomacy, eloquence, gracefulness, tact

Sarcasm: assertiveness, candor, contentment, kindness, sincerity

Selfishness: charity, consideration, generosity, helpfulness, restraint

Shyness: assertiveness, boldness, confidence, eloquence, helpfulness, initiative

Stealing: candor, contentment, fairness, respect, restraint, thoughtfulness

Stubbornness: consideration, flexibility, helpfulness, gracefulness, moderation, spontaneity, willingness

Thoughtlessness: artfulness, consideration, helpfulness, respect, thoughtfulness

Unfaithfulness: commitment, conviction, devotion, discipline, duty, gratitude, integrity, loyalty, restraint

Ungratefulness: contentment, gratitude, humility, respect, reverence

Appendix C

Practices

New ways of being do not come by reading about them, but through practice. It is not that practice makes perfect, rather that the perfection within you becomes visible through practice. To expand the expression of your soul, three suggested actions are listed below for each soul word. Calendar each practice for seven days, and at the end of twenty-one days you will have engrained a new way of being.

Acceptance:

- Before rising each morning, inhale deeply and consciously accept the breath of life into your body. Say aloud, "I accept the breath of life and am blessed with another day".

- Drive a heavily traveled route home from work or the store with an attitude of acceptance resulting from your *understanding* of the forces behind the traffic and the *order* in the situation.

- Daily accept an opportunity or gift offered to you.

Adoration:

- Adore animals and small children wherever you see them.

- Identify something or someone you adore every day and consciously acknowledge it to yourself.

- Find adorable traits in someone you've formerly deemed less than perfect.

Artfulness:

- Select a small area of your environment (the top of your dresser) and maintain it in an artful manner.

- Be artful about the presentation of all of your meals.

- Be artful in your manner of dress.

Assertiveness:

- When asked questions, give direct answers.

- Send in a letter to the editor about a topic upon which you have a strong opinion.

- Fully participate in a group discussion. Do not leave the discussion without saying all that you wish.

Benevolence:

- Compliment someone each day.

- Speak only well of everyone and all situations.

- Daily provide an opportunity for another person to succeed.

Boldness:

- Wear a bold article of clothing in public.
- Speak up for what you believe in a conversation or group discussion, especially if your opinion differs from the norm.
- In a group, be the first to do something such as sit, stand, speak, volunteer a new idea, agree or disagree.

Candor:

- When it is difficult to speak the truth, begin by saying "it appears to me...."
- Admit your mistakes without making excuses.
- Share a feeling with someone you trust.

Charisma:

- Sing in the shower.
- Ask someone to join you in an activity.
- Invite people to join your new discussion group.

Charity:

- Give money to a panhandler.

- Give away 10% of one paycheck to 7 donors by mailing a check a day to a charitable organization.
- Volunteer your time to a charity.

Cheerfulness:

- Skip twenty feet every day.
- Wish everyone you meet a nice day.
- Spend time in the morning imagining a good scene of some kind.

Cleverness:

- Daily, write ten uses for a bobby pin. Try writing some of them with your non-dominate hand.
- Observe things you find unusual.
- Find a clever solution to a long standing nagging situation.

Commitment:

- Make a simple daily commitment to yourself concerning health, work or relaxation.
- Write down all of your commitments, either formal or tacit and determine which are in conflict.
- Make a new commitment and reconcile your current agreements with it.

Compassion:

- In a meditative posture, recall painful moments in your past and send compassion to yourself.

- Note the pain of others expressed as anger or fear and apply love and understanding to them.

- Watch the nightly news and direct compassion toward all people involved (including the "bad" guys)

Confidence:

- List five things a day that you do with confidence regardless of how small they may seem. Read them aloud while smiling and facing a mirror.

- Make "I am" affirmations from soul words you strongly express and repeat them daily.

- Set a one week goal, and each day do something to accomplish it.

Consideration:

- Recognize when others directly do something to you that you do not like. Gently explain to them how their behavior makes you feel.

- Refrain from telling people what to do. Listen and ask them what it is they wish for themselves. Help them if you are able.

- Purchase and study a book dealing with

codependence. Take the actions discussed to establish healthy boundaries.

Contentment:

- Make a list and add to it daily of satisfying things in your life.

- Sit quietly and contently for three minutes a day.

- Observe a personally stressful situation to gain understanding of the forces at work. Become content with one aspect of the situation each day.

Conviction:

- Examine an area of your own life in which you wish to hold a strong conviction. List your basic beliefs supporting that conviction.

- Briefly describe your belief or a part of it to someone each day.

- Write a short essay on your new conviction or deliver a talk on the subject.

Courage:

- Create an imaginary situation in which you are in danger. Sit quietly with eyes closed for five minutes and see yourself confronting and overcoming the danger.

- Write an action plan for dealing with one of your fears.

- Carry out your action plan.

Creativity:

- Look at a picture of a single red rose daily. Close your eyes and see people giving you roses and when you receive them, feel filled with life.

- Wherever you drive, imagine your parking space is near the front door of your destination. Know that you have created it even before you arrive.

- Select a challenging situation from your life and imagine new possibilities for resolution. Daily take an action which creates a new, better situation.

Curiosity:

- Imagine for five minutes or more every day that you are a two year old child and see all of the things you would be curious about.

- Identify and list things you are curious about as an adult.

- Select one of the items from your list and pursue a path of discovery to learn all that you can about the subject.

Decisiveness:

- Identify a "problem" and list possible solutions along with the pros and cons for each one.

- Apply your judgment and make a decision about

how to solve the problem. List all of the actions needed to make your decision right.

- Use your strength to carry out the actions of your decision.

Devotion:

- List the people, things and ideas that you are strongly connected.

- Select from your list an item toward which you could enthusiastically dedicate yourself to sustain and nurture. List the actions that you can take to demonstrate your devotion,

- Carry out the actions listed.

Diligence:

- List in a left column areas of your life in which you desire diligence. Opposite each item in the right hand column, list the rewards for diligence in each area.

- Review your list and select areas for improvement. First list all of the possible rewards for becoming diligent and then write out an organization plan.

- Carry out your plan for diligence.

Diplomacy:

- In a family or work situation practice objectively listening to different points of view. Clarify your understanding with the speaker, but do not give your own opinion.

- Use opportunities to be a peacemaker by bringing together people in conflict and facilitating the discussion.

- In personal conflicts, use diplomacy to come to mutual agreements.

Discipline:

- Only use your non-dominate hand to drink. Record the number of times you accomplished this each day.

- Choose an exact time of day, say 9:00 pm, and each day read the lexicon discussion about the word "discipline".

- Write out your entire schedule for a week specifying work, eating, travel, recreation, reading, television, sleeping etc. Follow your schedule and note deviations.

Duty:

- In three columns list the following: first column, the roles that you accept responsibilities; second column, what you believe your duties are; third column, what others believe your duties are.

- Determine if there are differences between your acceptance of duties and other people's understanding of your duties. Identify conflicts in duties between different roles.

- Reconcile the conflicts by discussing the scope of your duties with interested parties and clarifying your agreement with them. Start with your highest obligation first and work down the list until no conflicts exist.

Eloquence:

- Describe who you are in twenty-five words or less. Repeat the practice daily, working to improve on the previous day's writing.

- Develop good speaking habits by speaking in complete sentences, eliminating "aha's","um's" and slang phrases such as "you know what I mean?"

- Organize and deliver a five minute speech to a club or friends introducing yourself to them.

Excellence:

- Select a routine task that you want to improve upon, and do it a little better each day.

- Create of list of the things you love to do or think you would love to do. Add to it daily.

- Select an item from your list and find small ways to improve it.

Fairness:

- Write a daily affirmation stating "I am ...." followed by a good trait you express. You may simply insert a soul word to complete the sentence, e.g. "I am fairness".

- List the times in your life when you have been unfair to yourself or others. Determine why you were this way and how you wish you had behaved. Do this gently, and with compassion for yourself.

- Select one of the items from your list to correct. Analyze the facts surrounding the situation and determine how to be more fair. Make amends.

Flexibility:

- Experience the joy of change by daily doing something completely new and unusual.

- Identify the things in your life you would like to release. Write them on a piece of paper and burn it, seeing yourself free from any connection to them.

- Use your power of imagination to determine with what you will replace those discarded ideas. Generate an abundant list of good to bring into your life. If any contrast with existing conditions, release the existing by writing them down and burning them.

Geniality:

- When greeting people ask them a question about themselves and show interest in their response by asking for more information.

- Take special time each evening to show interest in the members of your family. Show them that you like them.

- Be especially genial to the people in your place of work.

Generosity:

- Determine one thing that you have in abundance and give a portion of it away every day for a week.

- Determine something that you have very little of and and give a small portion away each day. Increase your giving as it is comfortable.

- With great enthusiasm, give away a rose a day to a complete stranger.

Gracefulness:

- Listen to your favorite music with eyes closed. Imagine yourself dancing or as an athletic performer executing your moves in complete gracefulness.

- Select a routine task in your private life and do it daily with focus and grace.

- Set aside a portion of your work day in which you

do everything with complete grace, resisting nothing and having total faith in yourself and the outcome.

Gratitude:

- Record how many times a day you say "thank you".

- List all of the good things you have in your life and compose a prayer of thanksgiving. Repeat the prayer daily.

- With this new awareness of the good in your life, verbalize your attitude of gratitude as often as possible.

Helpfulness:

- Ask one person a day "how may I be of service to you?" or "how may I help?"

- Look for opportunities to be helpful and feel loving as you perform the deeds.

- Maintain an attitude of service in all of your relationships with friends, family, work and community. Record each day how you were helpful.

Hope:

- Create a list of all of the circumstances within your sphere of influence you hope to improve.

- Select one of the items from your list that you believe you can change. Write a descriptive and highly detailed statement of a desirable future.

- Daily read your vision statement. Closing your eyes, see yourself in the picture as though it is happening now. Do actions which support your vision.

Humility:

- Pay attention to the words of others as though they have the answers to all of your questions.

- Ask your higher power to guide you out of difficult situations.

- Sit quietly in meditation for five minutes a day with a receptive attitude.

Humor:

- Look into the mirror and laugh. Do this daily for at least two minutes.

- Look for the possibility for humor in the situations and events which happen in your daily life. Write them down.

- Whenever you are angry or depressed find something in the situation which you find funny. Use this unique understanding to transform your attitude.

Initiative:

- List all of the things that you are waiting for. Determine what you can do to make them happen.

- Select from your list the most important thing you want to accomplish. Determine what you can do, independent of anyone else, to bring this about.

- Do it.

Integrity:

- Observe your daily actions and record every event that you feel conflicts with your ideals or makes you feel badly about yourself.

- Select a recurring issue from your list and meditate upon it daily, asking for divine guidance about how to be in integrity in the situation.

- Take the actions and make the changes suggested by spirit to establish your integrity on this issue.

Inventiveness:

- Look for situations in your world that could be improved with an invention. Be conscious of opportunities to be inventive.

- Determine that you will invent a solution to one of these situations. In a meditative and unbiased attitude, imagine many solutions to the problem, regardless of their practicality. Record them.

- Choose the best idea and develop the device you envisioned.

Kindness:

- Practice smiling and being gentle with everything in your world.

- Visit a convalescent hospital and spend time with people who rarely have visitors. See them as angels.

- Look for the good in everyone in your world and acknowledge it by radiating love to them.

Livelihood:

- List who, other than yourself, benefits from your productive activities. Determine which are chores for you and which are gifts from within your being.

- Select one of those chores and each day be conscious of its great value to others and ways it could express your essence as an individual. Whatever you do, see it as a service gladly given.

- Stop doing begrudging tasks and replace them only with those which your heart is in.

Loyalty:

- To know your own heart, list the principles by which you live your life. Determine if these are in alignment with your inner nature by asking if this "feels" correct.

- Reaffirm your loyalty to a single partner by coming to an understanding about the basic principles in your relationship. Write a statement of the principles upon which the relationship is based and post it for easy reference.

- Create a statement of principles with a group of three or more people at work, social or spiritual groups.

Mercy:

- Become aware of the ways in which you put down others. Correct that destructive action immediately by allowing space for them to express.

- Discover who in your life you hold down and keep in their place and determine what it is you fear in allowing them to be in power.

- Release your fears and encourage others to become self sufficient and come into their power.

Moderation:

- Determine what you are doing in excess. Fully write out the ultimate possible results of your actions and what moderate action you will take. Describe the ultimate results of moderation in this area.

- Create an affirmation for a new healthy desire to replace the excess and repeat it daily. For example, "I am vibrant and healthy. I treat my body well by feeding it wholesome, nourishing food."

- Overcome an irrational fear by applying reasonable caution and moderation.

Optimism:

- Upon awakening in the morning, imagine all of the good things which can happen for you.

- Whenever something "bad" happens, immediately think of some good which can come from it.

- Do not watch TV news, read the newspaper or expose yourself to negative programming for a full week. Notice how you feel.

Passion:

- Study your hand and observe how fantastic it is; then your eyes, and hair, your legs and feet. Become enthusiastic about your entire body and just being alive.

- List the routines in your life that you perform without conscious thought and no creativity. Determine how with a new attitude you can see each of these activities as creative.

- Each day find something to be really enthusiastic about. Become an enthusiastic creative participant in your routine actions.

Patience:

- Meditate five minutes daily on the three questions:

Who am I? Where am I going? How am I going to get there? Record your answers daily.

- Do a 500 piece jigsaw puzzle.

- Take at least 45 minutes a day to prepare your evening meal. Project your love into the food as you process is. Savor the meal, taking at least 15 minutes to eat it.

Perseverance:

- Compile a list of things you have wanted for yourself but have given up on.

- Determine which ones are important and think of ways to accomplish them.

- Choose a simple one and persevere to completion. If others remain important, include them in your goal planning.

Respect:

- Become aware of your actions that are designed to control others. Stop as soon as you recognize your behavior and allow people to choose for themselves.

- Listen to what other people are saying and acknowledge their right to say it.

- See how others attempt to control you. Protect your boundaries by saying "I respect your right to express an opinion, but that does not mean that I agree. I choose for myself".

Restraint:

- Do not gossip. Deflect conversation away from gossip, and excuse yourself from this type of conversation.

- Select one incident during your day in which you lacked restraint and reflect upon what is going on with you to cause this behavior.

- Choose any excessive behavior and use your inner powers of strength and renunciation to moderate it, or replace it with its opposite.

Reverence:

- Everyday, hold and revere something precious.

- See God in others and maintain a reverent attitude toward them.

- Look into a mirror. Close your eyes and revere what you feel.

Sentiment:

- Visit a museum and discover what most attracts your attention. What do these things mean in your memory?

- Daily play music which elicits a sentimental feeling: imagine you exist in other times with the music playing.

- Recognize and appreciate a person each day whom

you may have known in previous lives. Feel the warm sentiment.

Sincerity:

- Ask yourself at least three times a day "what am I feeling at this moment?" Learn to be in touch with your feelings.
- Do not lie or deceive anyone.
- Express your true feelings to someone at least once a day.

Sobriety:

- Change a small, harmless habit, such as which side of your face you shave first, or to which eye you first apply makeup.
- Abstain from a favorite food or drink.
- Replace watching television with fun activity.

Spontaneity:

- Drive home a different way every day. Set aside time one day to drive or walk spontaneously with no destination or route in mind. Observe what life shows you.
- Every evening, do something on the spur of the moment.
- Be alert for new opportunities offered to you daily. Do not judge their merits, but connect to your

inner feelings and if so guided, be spontaneous and do it.

Stewardship:

- Take care of something every day: balance your checkbook, wash your car, nurture your children, support your mate, or recycle waste products.

- Select the one thing in your life today that is most well cared for and meditate daily about what this symbolizes to you.

- Select one thing in your life that is falling apart. Establish a meaningful relationship and put love energy into it daily.

Tact:

- List your own emotional triggers, what makes you defensive, and avoid their use in your speech.

- Whenever you are critical of people, imagine their point of view to understand the behavior.

- Replace every demand you make of others with requests.

Thoughtfulness:

- Change your established morning routine for one week. See the expanded opportunities for discernment and decision making.

- Expand your consideration of others by

transcending thoughtlessness with judgment and will.

- Take action only after full deliberation. Ask "What are my choices, and what do I choose?"

Tolerance:

- List all of the things you dislike about yourself. Look at them as though they are attributes of an injured child and focus your loving attention upon healing.

- Notice how you project your personal intolerance upon others. Use love and compassion to become tolerant of their "imperfections".

- For a one hour period each day, shine love upon everything in your world. See some godliness in everything.

Valor:

- Once a day, as the opportunity presents itself, hold fast and refuse to do something that is against your inner guidance.

- What circumstance in your life most stifles your energy? Write out options for you to change these conditions.

- Face those fears and circumstances holding you down by calling upon your powers of life and strength to overcome them.

Vigor:

- Identify the activities in your life that tire you out. Find reasons to be enthusiastic and remind yourself of them as you perform the tasks.

- Write a list of all the things you love to do. Select one to do with vigor. Perform appropriate actions using strength and enthusiasm.

- Learn a new skill using all the strength and zeal you can muster.

Volition:

- Where do you feel most powerless? How did you give your power away? Identify how you can reclaim it.

- Notice how many times a day you let someone make decisions for you. At least once a day, decide for yourself.

- Own the results of your own decisions. Do not blame any condition on other people or outward circumstances.

Willingness:

- Look for opportunities all around you. Choose one a day and be willing to take it on.

- Discover what you refuse to do. What good do you forgo because of your reluctance?

- Select one thing you are reluctant to do that could be a joyful experience. Understand your fear, reframe the opportunity in this light and accept the challenge.

Wisdom:

- Daily pray or meditate with a receptive attitude. Be quiet and listen for the answer to your request.

- Expect answers to your prayers to show up in your life. Follow your intuition.

- Do not make rash decisions. Remain calm and call upon your inner judgment and understanding to guide you. Follow its advice.

Appendix D
Fundamentals of Expression

All of us in varying degrees speak the language of the soul. We speak the language when in some way we act upon the positive energy residing deep within us. There are literally hundreds of beneficial actions springing from the core of our being when we allow it. The system presented in this book identified sixty-six fundamental soul words. There are others, to be sure, but these particular words are connected directly to the twelve aspects of our divine nature.

Charles Fillmore, in his book <u>The Twelve Powers of Man</u>, describes in modern western vocabulary, twelve divine aspects that are within everyone; they make up the Christ within or Buddha nature, the essence of our being. These powers reside within us as potential energy and by combining with each other manifest through our physical being as the outer expression called the language of your soul. Every word in the lexicon is the working of two powers (shown italicized in the text) and soul word vocabulary is derived from all of the combinations of two out of the twelve powers listed below.

Following is a short explanation of each of the twelve powers:

Faith:

Faith enables us to move into uncharted areas while trusting in the outcome. It is our ability to say "yes' to a situation and move to confident action. Starting a new business or a new relationship is an act of faith. Without it, we would be frozen in inaction. We could not go to school, start families or embark upon careers. We could not participate in the community, nation or globe. In essence, faith is the trust we need to proceed into an unknown future.

Strength:

Strength enables us to persist and to do. It is our ability to sustain effort in the face of apparent opposition. Strength does not necessarily imply an overcoming of obstacles by force as in the case of physical strength, but can show up as non-resistance. Gandhi demonstrated tremendous strength by leading his people to national independence through peaceful means. Dr. Martin Luther King also demonstrated great strength asserting the need for equal rights while adhering to principles of non-violence.

Judgment:

Judgment is the ability to discern and choose rightly. It lets us see the consequences of various options and make an optimum choice. Judgment can develop with experience in people who are aware they are making choices and who actively learn during the course of their lives. Judgment is objective discernment without blame or shame.

Love:

Love is the energy system of the universe. It is the cosmic glue that binds us together. It is alternating current flowing to and fro between and among all the people of the world, and in fact all that is in creation. Love is the unifying principle of the universe. Relationships define our individuality, and we are who we are because of where we are. The where is described by our connection to other people and things. At the soul level, this connection is called love.

Power:

Power gives form to an idea. We transform our thoughts into written or spoken words. The "word" is then the power bringing thought into manifestation. An affirmation is a written or verbal commitment of our intentions. This may take the form of "affirmations" as used in spiritual practices, personal goal planning or more complex business plans. In all cases, we are putting an idea into motion by using words as the motive power.

Imagination:

Imagination is our ability to see new possibilities, to construct in the mind's eye things which never before existed. It is our ability to image. Great inventions of science, the arts, mathematics and social order all depend upon our ability to imagine new possibilities.

Zeal:

Zeal motivates us. It is the spark of enthusiasm that inspires us to action. It plays a role in most of our outer expression, for without interest in expressing ourselves we would become only observers of life. As souls we have chosen to incarnate into a physical body. The fact that we are here, in the physical universe is testament to the zeal coming from our soul.

Will:
Will is our ability to decide. It is through the use of will that we choose what it is we want. Will comes into play both when we institute new habits such as regular exercise and a balanced diet or cease old habits such as smoking and use of other harmful drugs. To make a change requires a decision. We encounter difficulty making a change when we have not really made a decision.

Renunciation:
Renunciation is the ability to let go--to say no. This faculty stands in contrast with faith which is our ability to say yes. Letting go is a large part of forgiveness. When we hold a grudge, no matter how much we love or understand, no matter how strong or wise, benevolent traits cannot be truly expressed. We must forgive and let go of blame and shame by invoking the power of renunciation.

Understanding:
Understanding is the ability to discern the fundamental truth of cause and effect. If we see the things and events in our world as symbolic of deeper meaning, understanding is our ability to get to that meaning. We need a basis for our beliefs and to know the relationship between the parts. This might be a scientific quest to know the workings of the physical universe, a study of psychology to comprehend human behavior, or an inward journey to

know ourselves. It is through our understanding that we come to know these relationships.

Life:

Life is the healing and regenerative power. It is the power animating us. Children are full of life, and were we to be "as the little children" we too could have this energy in our expression. The dull nature of many adults is not a question of chronological age, but how far they have distanced themselves from the life force. People radiate health who are tapped into the life force regardless of their age.

Order:

Order knows how to do things in their proper sequence. First things come first. We must sow before we can reap, chop wood before we can build a fire. A librarian organizes books and creates order to facilitate retrieval. A biologist has a classification system to catalog living things. A chef creates the order of mixing ingredients to produce a desirable outcome. All of these efforts call upon our faculty of order.